The Worry Stone

BY

Marianna Dengler

ILLUSTRATED BY

Sibyl Graber Gerig

rising moon

Books for Young Readers from Northland Publishing

The illustrations in this book were
rendered in watercolor and water color pencils
The display type was set in Ovidius
The text type was set in Perpetua
Composed by Northland Publishing, Flagstaff, Arizona
Printed and bound in Hong Kong by Wing King Tong Company Limited
Production supervised by Lisa Brownfield
Designed by Mary C. Wages
Art direction by Trina Stahl and Patrick O'Dell
Edited by Erin Murphy

FIRST IMPRESSION, September 1996
Second Printing, March 1997
ISBN 0-87358-642-5

Library of Congress Catalog Card Number 96-33837

Dengler, Marianna, 1935-
The worry stone / by Marianna Dengler ; illustrated by Sibyl Graber Gerig.
p. cm.
Summary: When a small, serious boy joins Amanda on the park bench, she remembers that once she was small and
serious too, but she had Grandfather—and his wonderful stories.
ISBN 0-87358-642-5
[1. Storytelling—Fiction. 2. Old age—Fiction. 3. Grandfathers—Fiction.
4. Chumash Indians—Fiction. 5. Indians of North America—California—Fiction.] I. Gerig, Sibyl Graber, ill.
II. Title.
PZ7.D4145Wo 1996
[E]—dc20   96-33837
                                                                                                       CIP
                                                                                                        AC
                                                                                                      REV

0661/10M/3-97

For Amy, the real-life Amanda,
and for Patti, who has a special gift for
finding worry stones. —M.D.

To my dear daughters,
Hannah, Adrienne, Emma,
and Madeline. —S.G.G.

A Note from the Author

Most folktales are handed down from one person to another, from generation to generation and even from century to century. Some, like *The Worry Stone*, come directly from the heart and mind of the storyteller.

Thus, the Chumash legend within this story is not authentic. I do hope, however, that it is consistent with the spirit of the People. For many years, I've walked their trails, joined their Solstice celebrations, and drawn strength from their mountains. I am grateful for their energy and their spirit, and I wish to pay them homage.

Many years ago my father gave me a worry stone and told a little bit about its power. A person who has one is nearly always considered fortunate, but there is widespread speculation and prodigious yarn-spinning regarding the origin of these magical stones.

Where does one look for worry stones? Along the edges of a country road. Along a path in the woods. Deep in the forest. Sometimes on the beach.

You'd think worry stones would be in streambeds, but I've rarely found them there. Where I've never found one is in the city, but that doesn't mean they're not there.

Worry stones can, of course, be anywhere. The thing is, you have to look for them. When you find a pebble that might be a worry stone, take it up and hold it and rub it. Trust yourself. You'll know if it feels different from an ordinary stone.

If you really want to find a worry stone, one will be waiting for you. I promise.

She lives in the Ojai Valley of California, where the weather is mild most all year round. Every day she walks to the park and sits for a while on a bench shaded by a sprawling oak. She carries a cane, and she wears a floppy old hat with a bright red feather.

Sometimes there are children in the park, and she loves watching them play and listening to their laughter. Her own children are grown and gone, scattered to the winds. When she counts the years, she knows she is old. When she looks around, she knows she is alone.

So she doesn't count, and she doesn't look around.

One afternoon a small boy comes and sits at the far end of the bench. His eyes are big and brown, and his face is serious. Much too serious, she thinks. She tries to talk with him, but though he stays for a long time, he never says a word.

The next day he is there again . . . and the next . . . just sitting quietly on the other end of the bench watching the other children. She likes having his company even though he doesn't talk.

Alone in her tiny room near the park, she thinks about the boy. His face is more than serious. It is sad. Why doesn't he smile? Why doesn't he laugh? Why doesn't he play with the others?

One day he speaks. "They won't play with me," he says.

"Why not?" she asks.

"I'm too little." He tries to sound matter-of-fact, but his voice quavers.

She nods, and the red feather dips over the brim of the floppy old hat. "You'll grow," she reassures him.

"So will they," he says with his clear child's logic. "I'll never catch up."

So it must seem, she thinks. Then, very gently, she asks, "Why do you come here?"

"Mama says I have to. Mama says I need air."

This time the red feather bobs up and down.

That night she is awake worrying about the boy. She knows exactly how he feels. Once, many years ago, she felt that way too.

But she had Grandfather.

She remembers it now as if it were yesterday.

ERS WAS A LARGE FAMILY, but no one had much time for Amanda except Grandfather, and no one had much time for Grandfather except Amanda, so they spent their days together.

The sprawling Spanish hacienda where they lived was surrounded by rolling hills and rich pasturelands. In the mornings Amanda and Grandfather took walks. In the afternoons they played checkers. And in the evenings they told stories— wonderful stories.

There were the really-truly stories of wild geese and ancient oaks. There were the passed-down stories of Indian princesses and Spanish *conquistadores,* and there were the spun stories, the ones she and Grandfather made up just as they went along.

These last ones always began, "Once upon a time, there was a beautiful child named Amanda who lived in a hacienda on the edge of time . . . "

Amanda was learning to tell the stories, trying out the pauses and scratchings of chin that made the suspense. She was not as good at it as Grandfather, but maybe someday she would be.

One morning in particular, Amanda and Grandfather set out on their walk as usual. Amanda lagged behind, searching the trail for things that might draw out one of Grandfather's stories.

A small pebble caught her eye. It was different from others she had found, so shiny it looked wet. She picked it up. It wasn't wet at all. How strange! Maybe Grandfather knew about it. He knew just about everything about everything.

She caught up with him on the path and thrust the pebble into his hand.

"Well, would you look at that!" Grandfather exclaimed, turning the pebble over and over, rubbing its smooth surfaces. "Haven't seen one of those in . . . forty years."

Amanda grew excited. "What is it?" she asked, dancing up and down.

He smiled mysteriously. "What does it look like?"

"A little rock," she said, taking it into her hand.

He raised his eyebrows, and she knew he expected a better answer than that.

She tried again. "An arrowhead?"

"Nope."

She studied the pebble. "A fossil." Grandfather had told her all about fossils, and she was looking closely for impressions left by leaves or insects.

"Nope," he said again, and with that he went striding on down the trail.

She grasped the pebble firmly and hurried after him. Maybe tonight there would be a brand new story.

That afternoon she was so excited she could hardly keep her mind on the checkers, and Grandfather whomped her three games running. At dinner she was so impatient she could hardly eat.

Later, on the veranda, she stood first on one foot and then on the other, waiting for the story.

Would it be an old one?

Some of the tales she knew by heart. Most of them she'd heard many times, but once in awhile, there was a brand new story, one she'd never heard before. Amanda loved them all, but tonight she hoped it would be a new story, the story of the little pebble.

Grandfather stalled, just as he always did, taking his own sweet time getting settled. First he wanted his slippers. Then he wanted tea. Then he needed lemon. Then he asked for honey.

Amanda fetched them all.

At last Grandfather lifted her into his lap, and she snuggled into the crook of his arm. She was happy. Any story would do, but just as a reminder, she put the pebble into his hand.

Grandfather turned it over and over, studying it. Then he rubbed it . . . and rubbed it . . . and rubbed it until Amanda thought he was never going to stop.

"This," he said finally, "is not a pebble at all."

"It looks like a pebble," Amanda said.

"A worry stone. That's what it is."

"A worry stone?" Amanda looked closer.

Grandfather nodded. "The real thing."

Amanda took it and rubbed its surfaces with her fingertips as Grandfather had done. There were little hills and valleys, but no sharp edges. It was an irregular shape, but so smooth it felt almost soft.

"Folks say these stones have special powers," he said.

"Powers?" Amanda could hardly contain herself. "What kind of powers?"

Grandfather scratched his chin. "Well, folks say if you're troubled or worried . . . and if you rub the stone gently, like this . . . the worry goes away."

Amanda searched Grandfather's face. When he started with "Folks say . . . " she knew it was a passed-down story.

"Does it really work?" she asked.

"Always has for me," he said.

"You have one?"

"Used to. Gave it away some years back to a fellow who needed it more."

"Where do they come from?" Amanda asked. She had learned how to ask the right questions.

"Well now," Grandfather said, settling back and getting that faraway look in his eye.

At last, the story began.

Long, long ago, before the white man came, there lived an Indian maiden of the peaceful Chumash tribe. Her name was Tokatu (Dove), and she loved only Akima (Black Bear).

To their great joy and in accordance with the custom of their people, the marriage of Akima and Tokatu was arranged. Then a shadow fell across their happiness. Three days before the wedding, a hostility arose between two rival branches of the tribe. A sacred code of honor had been violated, and within hours the entire Chumash nation was swept into a brief but bloody civil war.

All the young men of the village were called into battle, and so Akima went with the others. For three days Tokatu kept a vigil, but Akima did not return.

Before daylight on the day of the wedding, Tokatu put on the ceremonial dress. The marriage was to take place at dawn, and still Akima had not come. All day, she kept watch, but it was not until dusk that the young men of the village returned. They came bearing Akima on a litter. Tokatu knelt beside the litter, and at Akima's word, the ceremony began.

The couple spoke the ancient vows and drank from the Cup of Life. Then, as the braves of the village danced around them, the Wind of Time carried off Akima's spirit.

Tokatu lived long among her people, but she took no other husband. She wove baskets of great beauty, and she grew wise, holding a seat of honor at the council fire.

Each year on the anniversary of Akima's death, Tokatu put on the ceremonial dress and went alone to his place of rest. Each year she prayed that someday his spirit and hers would be united. Each year she wept and could not stop weeping. Her tears fell one by one until Mother Earth was wet.

At last, when Tokatu was old, the Wind of Time came for her. As was their custom, the women of the village took her body to its place of rest beside Akima. There they found his grave covered over by small, smooth pebbles like none the women had seen anywhere within the range of their moccasins.

"These are the Tears of Tokatu," they said. "Lest we forget, let us each take one back to the village."

In time, it was discovered that great troubles were eased by the rubbing of the Tears of Tokatu, and the stones became much sought after by the People.

Tokatu had wept for all of them.

As the years passed, the power of the stones was reported from as far away as the Mission of San Diego, but the lovers were forgotten. The Tears of Tokatu, like the Chumash themselves, were scattered.

Because people no longer knew the story, they simply called them worry stones.

Grandfather paused then, looking down at Amanda. "Even today, those who find a worry stone are very fortunate. No matter what their trouble, they will be comforted."

Amanda sat silent, secure in her grandfather's arms. The story had left her thoughtful, but not sad. She still had the worry stone in the hollow of her hand.

"Am I fortunate?" she asked.

"You are," he said. "There aren't many worry stones left."

The wonder of the story lay upon her for days, and she kept the worry stone with her, trying it out on such little things as games of checkers and the like, but it didn't seem to work. One day she left it on her dresser, and finally she tucked it into a velvet locket box and forgot about it.

One night while Amanda was asleep, the Wind of Time came for Grandfather.

In the morning Amanda was told what had happened.

She did not cry. She only walked out on the veranda and sat in Grandfather's chair. Her heart was numb, but in time the numbness gave way, and like Tokatu, she wept and could not stop the tears from falling.

One evening at story time, she went to her dresser and opened the velvet locket box. She took up the worry stone. Still weeping, she rubbed its smooth surfaces, and after a while, she fell asleep.

That night she dreamed of Grandfather, of their morning walks, of their afternoon games of checkers, of their stories. It was a long, sweet, beautiful dream, and when she awoke, she knew that Grandfather would be with her always.

The worry stone was still in the hollow of her hand. Its power was real.

In her tiny room near the park, she sits upright in bed. She
knows now what she can do for the boy on the bench. Though
it is very early in the morning, she fumbles for her cane and
moves quickly across to the dresser.

Her hands tremble as she rummages through the drawers,
until finally she finds what she is looking for—the velvet
locket box.

That afternoon she waits on the park bench for the boy. He
is late. Maybe he won't come. Maybe he will never come again.

She thinks of Grandfather and of the child, Amanda, who
lived in the hacienda on the edge of time. He on the one side;
she on the other. So happy together.

Then she sees the boy coming toward her.

"Sit over here today," she suggests, patting the space on the
bench beside her.

"Why?" He stands a few paces away, undecided.

"I have something to show you." She opens her hand. In it is
the small pebble.

The boy comes up. "What's that?" he asks.

"What does it look like?"

"A little rock," he says.

She can feel his disappointment. "Nope," she says.

"Then what is it?" he asks.

Now it's her turn to be disappointed, but, of course, he doesn't know how to play the game.

"This," she says, "is a real, genuine worry stone."

"Oh." He is not impressed.

They are both silent.

She tries again. "Some say these stones have special powers." She waits.

And she waits.

"What kind of powers?" he asks.

"Well, they say if you're troubled or worried, and if you rub the stone gently, like this, the trouble will go away."

She rubs the stone. First, between her fingers. Then, between the palms of her hands. The boy watches. Then he looks away.

"I don't believe it," he says flatly.

"It works for me," she tells him.

His eyes are full of doubt. "Really?"

She nods so hard the red feather on the floppy old hat nearly touches her nose.

The boy edges closer, standing beside her examining the stone. "Where did it come from?" he asks.

"Well now," she says, leaning forward. "A long, long time ago, there was an Indian maiden named Tokatu . . . "

She tells the story of the worry stone simply, but she remembers to pause in all the right places, and once, to increase the tension, she even scratches her chin.

The boy beside her is quiet, looking back and forth from her face to the small pebble in her hand.

"Even today," she says, "those who have a worry stone are fortunate. No matter what their trouble, they will find comfort."

"Are you fortunate?" he asks.

"I am," she says. "And now you are, too."

With that, she puts the worry stone into his small hand.

"For me?"

She nods.

He sits on his end of the bench and goes back to watching the other children play, his face just as sad as ever. Forgotten, the worry stone falls to the ground.

For the first time in her life, Amanda feels old and very much alone. She looks away, too sad to stay longer but too tired to start home.

"Where did you get it?" the boy asks. He has picked up the stone and is turning it over and over in his hands, rubbing its smooth surfaces just as she has done.

"I found it," she says.

"Where?" he asks.

"Not far from here."

"How do you know about it?"

"My grandfather," she says. "He told me the story of Tokatu."

The boy moves toward her on the bench. "Did he have any other stories?"

"Many stories," she says. "Wonderful stories."

How well she remembers them—the really-truly stories of wild geese and ancient oaks, and the passed-down stories of Indian princesses and Spanish *conquistadores,* and the spun stories, the ones she and Grandfather made up as they went along.

"Will you tell me another story?" the boy asks.

Amanda looks at the boy for a long moment. It's time to stall, but she can't very well ask for slippers and tea. "Maybe, sometime," she says.

"It's okay," he says. "You don't have to."

"Tomorrow," she suggests.

"Now?" he asks. "Please?"

"Well," she says, taking a deep breath. "Don't know if I can remember."

"You can." He moves closer, but he's still half a bench away.

"What if I get stuck?" she asks. "Will you help?"

He nods and moves on over until he's sitting right beside her. Amanda smiles down at him.

"Once upon a time," she begins, "there was a handsome child named . . . named . . . "

The boy looks up, catches the twinkle in her eyes.

"Jason," he says.

"Jason," she says.

The bright red feather dances up and down, and the boy smiles.

About the Author

One night, after the death of her father, MARIANNA DENGLER found her daughter, Amy, asleep with a worry stone in her hand. Holding the stone gave her dreams about her grandfather, she said, which made her feel close to him and made losing him less painful. This gave Marianna the idea for *The Worry Stone*. But it was Patti, Amy's older sister, who insisted that this story be told.

Marianna has written several books and also writes for television and feature film: She has optioned a two-part miniseries for television, has written four screenplays, and has helped create a pilot for Children's Television Workshop.

Marianna lives in Westlake Village, California, with her husband, Ben. Her favorite pastimes are good movies, starlight concerts, folk music, and reading at night when everyone else is asleep. She looks forward to welcoming her first grandchild, who is due as this book goes to press.

About the Illustrator

SIBYL GRABER GERIG was born in St. George, Pribilof Islands, Alaska. She spent her childhood and adolescent years in Aibonito, Puerto Rico. Since then she has lived in Virginia, Ohio, and England. She now lives in Mishawaka, Indiana, with her husband, Winston, and their four daughters, Hannah, Adrienne, Emma, and Madeline.

Sibyl completed her undergraduate training at Goshen College in northern Indiana and received an MFA in medical and biological illustration from the University of Michigan. She has illustrated numerous journal and magazine articles, books, and medical texts. She feels her training in medical illustration, which involved many careful, realistic renderings, lent itself well to the detailed portraiture in her first children's book, *The Underbed* (Good Books), and in *The Worry Stone*.